Garey -

merry reading

and learning!

Christmas 1991

Love you lots!

mom & Dad

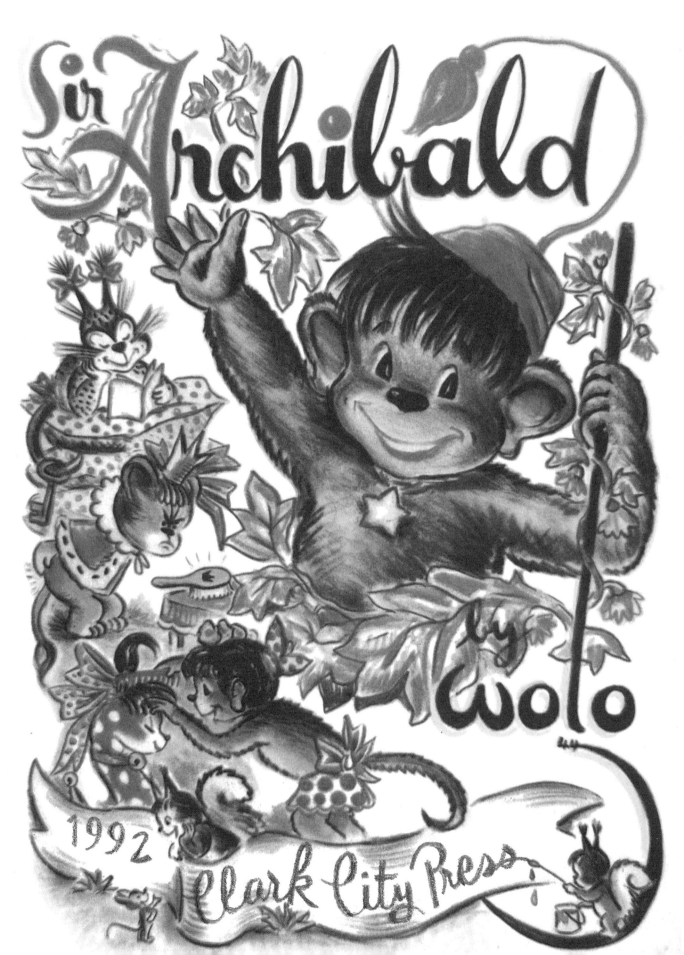

LIBRARY OF CONGRESS CATALOG CARD NUMBER: 91-73411

ISBN: 0-944439-22-5

Color separations by Spectrum West, Inc.
Printed and bound in the U.S.A. by Ringier America, Inc.

Clark City Press
POST OFFICE BOX 1358
LIVINGSTON, MT 59047

Some thing terrible had happened. The lion King's brand new crown was missing! He'd taken his noonday nap and when he woke up it was GONE!

Needless to say all the animals were in an uproar. Sir Woebegone, the King's privy councillor, was simply frantic, and the Queen had left in tears to have a royal headache.

The only one who wasn't upset was the King himself. "Frankly speaking," he said, "I don't mind one bit. In fact, I'm rather pleased the big old thing is gone. It was heavy and it was itchy—especially on hot days!"

But, Sir Woebegone felt otherwise. "A thousand pardons, Your Majesty," he replied. "But, if I be permitted to say so, a King must never be without a crown. It is most unroyal. It simply is not done! I, for one, sha'n't rest until it is safely back on your noble head!"

"All right, all right!" grumbled the King. "I'll put the crown on again—if you find it. Meantime, don't lose any feathers over it!" Then he added, "but I certainly would like to know who took it!"

"I have my suspicions!" whispered the privy councillor nervously. "Of course, I don't know, but I'd say it was Grizzlegrimm and his Meanies!" For, you see, whenever the animals didn't know who to blame for a wicked deed, they just blamed Grizzlegrimm!

"Hmm," said the King, thoughtfully. "Have you asked everybody?"

"Everybody but Miss Miff, the gossipy old buglebird," replied Sir Woebegone.

"Well, where is she?" asked the King. "She usually knows everything!"

"Oh, she's out having tea with some guinea-hens—probably talking her feathers off," said Sir Woebegone. "There's no telling when she'll be back!"

"Well, send one of the rabbits after her!" said the King impatiently. But just then Miss Miff, the buglebird, came fluttering in with her pink parasol and her knitting and looking very red in the face.

"Dearie-me!" she cackled. "I flew back as soon as I heard about it, and—well now—of course, I'm not saying anything, but if you ask ME, I'd say it was Grizzlegrimm

and his Meanies took the crown. Come to think of it, I believe I saw him around only this morning. Yes, I'm sure I saw him take something and run away with it—I think. Well, anyway, I'm certain it was he!"

"You see! It's just as I thought!" whispered the privy councillor to the King. "It's just as I thought!" But when he turned to the animals and asked them who would be brave enough to get the crown back, they just hung their heads and one by one slipped away, for they were all scared to death of Grizzlegrimm.

"What a mess!" sighed Sir Woebegone. "What a mess!" It looked as if the King would never wear his crown again.

Now, there lived not very far
away, in a leaf-house upon a tree,
a little monkey. His name was Sir
Archibald. When he heard what had happened, he said to
himself, "I am not afraid! I shall go and get that crown back,
and fight Grizzlegrimm! I'll tear him to pieces—little teenie
pieces! I'm not scared of anything in the whole world!"

Then he cut himself a big stick, and said good-by to
his friend, Amanda, the kind little polka-dot snake, who
lived right down-stairs below his tree, and went on his way
to see the King.

"What a lovely day!" he thought to himself. Twirling his stick he scampered along until he came close to the King's palace. There he met Floribel, the Queen's monkey-in-waiting, out for a walk with Princess Trundlebumps, the lion King's little daughter.

"How do you do?" said Sir Archibald politely and, after they had told each other their names, he asked her would she please show him the way to the royal palace.

"I'll gladly take you there," replied Floribel. "But I tell you right now, if it's the King you want to see, it had better be something very important! He's just been listening to a delegation of pea-hens—for two hours, mind you! They nearly drove him crazy. Then he had to settle an argument between two skunks and one of them lost his temper. So, you see, His Majesty is a bit upset this morning!"

By this time they had reached the court, and Floribel said, "There you are." "I see," said Sir Archibald. He thanked her, and then walked cheerfully right up to the throne.

When the lion King saw him he roared: "NOW what? First it's pea-hens, then it's skunkers, and now I suppose it's monkey-business! Anyway, pray tell us, who are you and what can I do for you?"

"My name is Sir Archibald," answered the little monkey, bowing courteously. "I have come to fight Grizzle-grimm and get your crown back!"

When the King heard that, he was very much impressed. "What a brave little fellow!" he said.

"A most courageous person, indeed!" chimed in Sir Woebegone. "You're really not afraid to fight him?"

"I'm not scared of anything in the whole world!" answered Sir Archibald. "Just tell me where I can find him."

"He lives on the Black Rock by the sea," replied the King, and turning to his privy councillor, he asked him: "I say, haven't we got a map of the place around here somewhere?"

"I'll go and see, Your Majesty," said Sir Woebegone, and he soon returned with several big charts which he unrolled with great dignity. The first one was a map of the land of the Hippopotamussers. "That's not the one," said Sir Woebegone, adjusting his glasses. Next came a map of the Stork Island. "It's a lovely place," he said, "but it's not what we're looking for right now." The next showed the country where the red-faced baboons lived. Then came a map of the Queen's vegetable garden. And finally the map of the Black Rock by the sea where Grizzlegrimm lived!

"It would be the very last one," said the King in a very impatient voice.

"Of course," replied Sir Woebegone. "I was quite certain it would be.

"Then why didn't you pick it right away?" asked Sir Archibald.

"Because, then it would have been the first one," sighed Sir Woebegone. "It's to teach us patience."

"Now, then," he said, "the place is not hard to find. First, you come to the Eerie - Woods - of - the - Gnarled Trees - with - the - Roots - in - the - Air. Then come the Scarey Stumps. After that the desert and the Narrow Valley where nobody has ever been — and then the Threadneedle Pass with the iron gate. That's where Bee-sark the Snifferpuss lives. She's the only one who has the key to the gate."

"Beesark the WHAT?" asked Sir Archibald.

"Beesark the Sniffer-puss!"

"And what does she do?"

"That's just it," continued the privy councillor. "You never can tell! Anyway, if she doesn't let you go through the Threadneedle Pass, it's just too bad, because on the other side is the Black Rock by the sea where Grizzlegrimm lives! And that," he said, carefully rolling up the map, "is all." Then he added, politely, "I do wish you luck!"

"As do I!" said the King.

But Sir Archibald stuck out his little chest and shouted, "Don't you worry about me. I'm not afraid of anything in the whole world!"

And with that, he was on his way to the Black Rock by the sea to fight Grizzlegrimm and the Meanies!

Everything went well until, toward nightfall, he came to the Eerie-Woods-of-the-Gnarled-Trees-with-the-Roots-in-the-Air.

"It does look spooky in there," he thought. "But I'm not afraid of anything in the whole world!"

Just then he heard a noise —and he stopped.

There were three Mean-
ies peeking at him from be-
hind the trees. "Woo-hoo!
Woo-hoo!" they shouted.
"BEWARE!
The Eerie Woods are full of fears.
The Blinky Owls will nip your ears.
Eerie whack—TURN BACK!"

When Sir Archibald heard that, he began to feel
goosel-bumpy and cold all over! "Jeepers!" he cried,
and he turned about face and he ran, and he ran, and
he ran until he was right back where he started from!

13

And then he stopped and sat down and buried his face in his paws—for he was terribly ashamed of himself. "It's a good thing it is getting dark," he thought. "I'll tip-toe past the King's court and go and hide some place where nobody is ever going to see me again!" But just as he got up he saw somebody coming toward him.

It was Floribel, on her way to the river, to get a drink of water for Princess Trundlebumps. The Princess had just been put to bed and, you know how it is, little girls always ask for a drink of water just when you think they are asleep. "Why, it's Sir Archibald!" she said, coming nearer. "What's happened?"

"The Meanies scared me!" he answered. "They scared me and chased me back! And here I told the King I wasn't afraid of anything in the whole world. Oh! How can I ever look anybody in the face again?"

"Poor Sir Archibald," soothed Floribel. "It really isn't as bad as all that. Don't you know that nobody can be a hero unless he first knows what it is to be afraid? The main thing is to try again!

The Meanies can only hurt those who are afraid of them. Don't listen to them. Don't even look at them and they will never harm you!" And then she said, "Tell me, where did you get the pretty little star around your neck?"

"I found it one day when I climbed a high mountain," answered Sir Archibald.

"It's magic!" said Floribel. "Anyone who finds his star need never be afraid any more!"

"What do you mean?" asked the monkey.

"Just this," said Floribel, "and remember it now! Whenever you're afraid *just hold onto your little star* and everything will be all right!"

Sir Archibald thought a little while, and then he jumped up and stuck out his chest and said, "Very well! I'll go back right now and try it again!"

"I knew you would," replied Floribel. "And I'm proud of you. But I'd wait 'til morning. It's getting much too dark to find your way."

Sir Archibald agreed, and when Floribel had gone back to the Princess, he curled up in the high grass and soon was fast asleep, holding onto his little star.

Early the next day—before anybody else was up —Sir Archibald was on his way. "I'm truly not afraid of anything this morning," he said to himself. But when he came to the Eerie Woods, the trees looked just as spidery and fearful as ever. "I only wish I didn't have to go through here," he whispered to himself.

Suddenly there were the three Meanies again, growling and scowling at him from behind the trees. The first one said, "You'll surely get lost!" The second one said, "You'll surely die of hunger and thirst!" The third one cried, "You'll never get through!" And then they all rushed at him shouting:

"Eerie whack! Eerie whack! Turn back! Turn back!
The Spider Trees are full of fears.
The Blinky Owls will nip your ears.
Eerie whack—TURN BACK!"

Poor little Sir Archibald was just about to run away again when he remembered what Floribel had told him, and so he held onto his little star and shouted:

"Don't hear you,
Don't see you,
You're nothing to me;
And how in the world
Can a nothing stop me!"

He had no sooner said so when all the Meanies disappeared! Sir Archibald was very much surprised. "Well!" he said to himself. "It certainly worked." And sticking out his chest, he went on through the Gnarled-Trees-with-the-Roots-in-the-Air. He did meet some owls, but they were all very nice to him, bidding him the time of day. One of them even wished him a pleasant journey! "Thank you!" he said. "It's most kind of you."

And he went through the woods until he heard a strange buzzing noise. It was the Scarey Stumps! The closer he came to them, the angrier they buzzed.

"Oh dear, oh dear!" sighed
the little monkey. "Those ragged
stumps do look spooky. I only wish
I didn't have to go through here!"

Right then the Meanies were there
again—rushing at him and shouting:

"Woo-hoo! Woo-hoo! You'll never get through!
The Scarey Stumps are full of bats,
And Woolleywickedwhatnots.
Habee! Haboo! You'll never get through!"

Sir Archibald nearly, nearly became fright-
ened again, but then he quickly said:

"Don't hear you.
Don't see you.
You're nothing to me,
And how in the world
Can a nothing *scare me?"*

And all the Meanies disappeared again!

"Well!" said the little monkey. "It works just like magic." And he went right ahead. When he came to the Scarey Stumps, he found nothing there to frighten him. There were a few bats, all of them asleep, and as for the buzzing noise—it was just some wild bees busily gathering honey!

"Those silly Meanies," he mumbled to himself. "To think that they scared me once!"

He went on until he came to the desert. "It's certainly getting hot," he thought. "What's more, I'm thirsty as can be—and hungry, too; but I'm not going to stop for anything." And he bravely plodded on.

Suddenly he saw something ahead of him. At first he thought it to be a Meanie but it turned out to be a big and very fat bird, sitting on a rock and looking dreamily into the sky. Sir Archibald bade him the time of day, but the strange bird never even noticed him. Just then he heard a small thin voice saying, "You mustn't bother him! You really mustn't!" It was a little desert mouse peeking out from his burrow beneath the rock.

"Why? What's the matter with him?" asked Sir Archibald.

"He's thinking about the Whys - and - Wherefores," said the desert mouse.

"And why should anyone worry about them?" asked Sir Archibald.

"I'm sure I don't know!" sighed the mouse. "He's been sitting there for ever-so-long, and the longer he sits, the fatter he gets. If he worries much longer he won't be able to fly any more!"

"He's in a bad fix," said Sir Archibald. "May I ask what

21

you are doing here?"

"Who? Me?" asked the little mouse. "Why I'm waiting for him to tell me!"

"Tell you WHAT?" asked Sir Archibald.

"I'm waiting for him to tell me about the Whys-and-Wherefores, silly!" replied the mouse impatiently. "Now run along, the morning is half gone and he's barely begun to think!"

"Goodness me!" said Sir Archibald, shaking his head. "The way some people spend their time!" And he went on his way again, wondering what he'd see in the Narrow Valley where nobody has ever been.

He found it to be a lovely place, with lush green meadows and date-palms, little fat bushes full of juicy red berries, and a cool spring.

Sir Archibald quenched his thirst and ate his fill. "Well," he thought, resting up a bit, "everything's been going very well, indeed! I didn't die of hunger or thirst, the owls didn't nip my ears, and I most certainly didn't lose my way! As for the Woolleywickedwhatnots—those Meanies are the biggest fibbers ever! I don't know why anyone should be afraid of them!" And he grabbed a paw-full of red berries to munch on the way. He soon came to the Threadneedle Pass.

There sat Beesark the Snifferpuss. "It's about time you were here!" she said curtly. "The gate's been open for an hour!"

"How did you know I was coming?" asked Sir Archibald.

"I can always sniff 'em coming!" said Beesark. "When they smell good to me I let 'em through. And when they don't—I EAT 'EM! Now run along."

"I see," replied Sir Archibald, scurrying through the Pass.

When he came on the other side
he saw the Black Rock by the sea.
"What a creepy place!" thought Sir
Archibald. An icy wind was blowing in his face, and
there, right in front of him, stood the dreaded Grizzlegrimm surrounded by a whole swarm of screaming
Meanies!

"Beware! Turn Back!" one cried. "He'll squash
you like a flea!" warned another. "He'll tear you to
pieces!" screamed a third. "Habee—Haboo—he'll
surely get you!" chanted a fourth. The only one who
didn't say anything was old Grizzlegrimm himself.
He just scowled at him with his great big eyes!

Poor Sir Archibald felt gooselbumpy all over — but he stood his ground. Oh, he was terribly brave! And then he lifted his big stick, and holding onto his little star, he shouted as loud as he could:

"You're just a lot of nothings
And you can't scare me,
I've promised to fight you
And I'll do it—you'll see!"

In a flash all the Meanies were gone and then suddenly the big thing happened. The mighty Grizzlegrimm *slowly fell over on his back!* At first the little monkey could hardly believe his eyes. Then he came nearer, and he found to his amazement that the great and terrible Grizzlegrimm everybody had been scared to death of — was only a DUMMY! A dummy MADE OF STRAW!

"Well can you imagine that?" said Sir Archibald. "So he was nothing but a big scare-crow—and we let the Meanies worry us about him until we believed he was a real live thing!" And he laughed and laughed!

Then he hunted for the King's crown. He hunted all over and around the Black Rock, but of course he couldn't find it. "How could a dummy steal a crown?" he thought. "It must have been somebody else. But I'm too tired to worry about that now!" So he picked up Grizzlegrimm— he wasn't heavy at all—and carried him through the Threadneedle Pass. The gate was still open and Beesark the Snifferpuss asked no questions. So he hurried past her with a smile and a "thank you!" and went down into the Narrow Valley. There he stretched out beneath a shady tree and went peacefully to sleep, using Grizzlegrimm for a pillow.

Back at the King's court the Queen was sitting under a mulberry tree, having her mane brushed by Floribel while the little Princess played nearby. She seemed to be eating something, and when Her Majesty noticed this, she said: "Trundlebumps! How many times does Mother have to tell you not to put things into your mouth? Come right here and show me what it is!" But Trundlebumps wouldn't come—she just stood there pouting.

"Very well!" said her Mama sternly, "Floribel! give me the royal hairbrush!" When the little Princess heard that she slowly came nearer, opening her mouth. What do you think was in it? "Why it's the big red ruby from the King's crown!" gasped the Queen. And then she cried,

"Trundlebumps! WHERE IS PAPA'S CROWN?"

Trundlebumps told them. The crown had dropped from the King's head while he was taking his nap, and she had broken off the big red ruby on top 'cause it looked just like a lolly-pop. Then using the crown as a cradle, she had put her pussycat to sleep in it and hidden it beneath the throne!

27

"And why didn't you tell us about it?" asked her mother, sternly.

"'Cause—I just DID-N'T!" answered Trundle-bumps, pouting and looking as saucy as can be.

"Why you naughty little girl!" said the Queen, and she gave Trundle-bumps a good spanking with the royal hairbrush for all the trouble she had caused.

And so the crown was found. The King put it on again, with a sigh. Sir Woebegone was delighted and most relieved, but Floribel ran straight to Miss Miff's and gave her a piece of her mind.

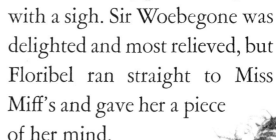

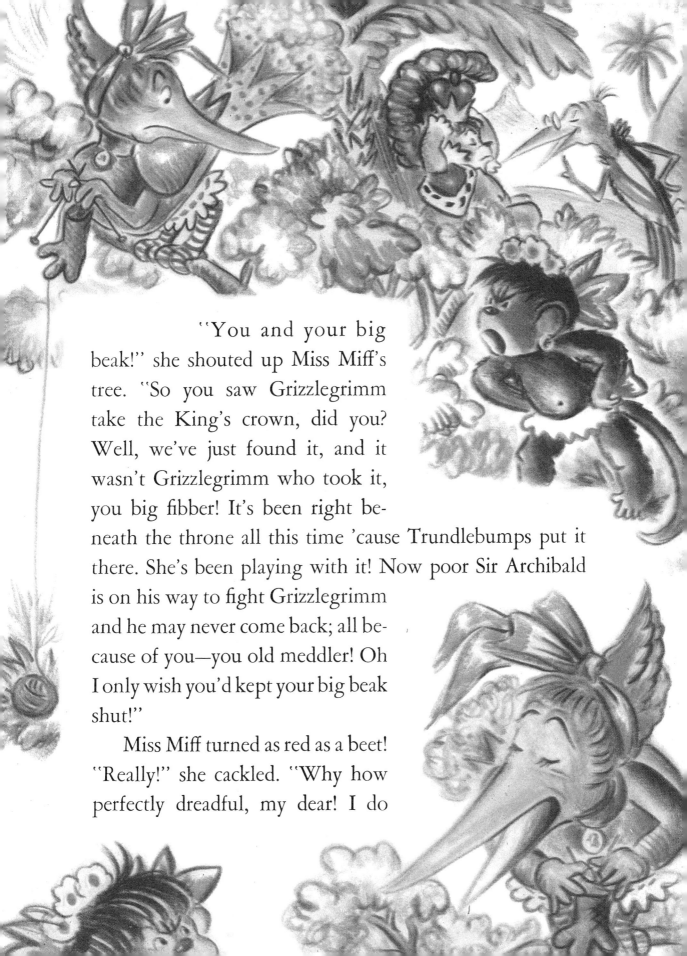

"You and your big beak!" she shouted up Miss Miff's tree. "So you saw Grizzlegrimm take the King's crown, did you? Well, we've just found it, and it wasn't Grizzlegrimm who took it, you big fibber! It's been right beneath the throne all this time 'cause Trundlebumps put it there. She's been playing with it! Now poor Sir Archibald is on his way to fight Grizzlegrimm and he may never come back; all because of you—you old meddler! Oh I only wish you'd kept your big beak shut!"

Miss Miff turned as red as a beet! "Really!" she cackled. "Why how perfectly dreadful, my dear! I do apologize! It must have been my eyes, they've been bothering me quite a bit lately. Dear me! Sir Archibald is in a PREDICAMENT, isn't he! Goodness gracious! Just to show you that my heart's in the right place, I'll fly off this minute and see if I can call him back."

"That's very nice of you indeed!" said Floribel. "Thank you very much. I'm sorry about what I said right now—about your big beak."

"That's quite all right, my dear!" replied the bugle-bird. "It IS big, and there isn't a thing can be done about it!" With that she put down her knitting and promptly flew away to look for Sir Archibald.

She had quite a time, but finally she found him trudging through the Narrow Valley, whistling merrily and dragging Grizzlegrimm's dummy behind him.

"YE POTS AND LITTLE PIE-PANS!" she cried. "There he is AND HE'S KILLED GRIZZLEGRIMM! I can hardly believe my eyes!" So she swooped down and hurriedly told Sir Archibald that the crown had been found. " 'Twas the little Princess," she cackled. "She's been playing with it!" And before he could open his mouth she was off again to rush back with the great news of Sir Archibald's victory.

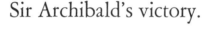

Now when the King and everybody heard what Sir Archibald had done they shouted for joy. His Majesty sent Arabella, his fastest giraffe to carry him back! You should have seen her go! Swish through the Eerie Woods, swish past the Scarey Stumps, swish—swish across the desert, 'til she met him just as he came out of the Narrow Valley.

"I bring you the King's greetings!" she shouted, panting something awful, "the King's most royal greetings!" She was all out of breath! "His Majesty asks me to bring you back right away—everybody is waiting for you!"

"That certainly is most kind of him," answered Sir Archibald. "But you really must have a drink of water

first!'' So he led her to the cool
spring in the valley where Arabella
quenched her thirst. Then the little monkey loaded Grizzlegrimm on Arabella, jumped on himself and swish — they
were off on their way back!

Floribel was the first to meet them. She had been anxiously waiting ever since Arabella had left. "It's so good to see you back safely!" she cried. "And now you're a real hero!" "Oh, it really wasn't much," replied Sir Archibald, modestly, for he had learned never to brag again. "If it weren't for what you told me about the Meanies and my little star, I could never have done it at all! And now, please hold out your paws, and close your eyes—tightly!"

Floribel did, and when she opened them again, she found he'd given her something wrapped up in a big leaf, with a lovely flower on top. "It's some red berries I gathered for you in the Narrow Valley. The flower is for you to put in your hair—and to smell pretty!"

"How sweet of you!" said Floribel. "Thanks ever so much! But now you must hurry, for the King and everybody are waiting. I'll run ahead and tell him you're coming!"

"All right," replied Sir Archibald. "But first I'd better tidy up Arabella a bit—she looks a sight!"

And then Sir Archibald came prancing in while everybody cheered! He jumped off Arabella and bowed and, tossing Grizzlegrimm at the King's feet, he said, "Here he is, Your Majesty!"

Now when the King and Sir Woebegone saw Grizzlegrimm, they looked and looked 'til their eyes nearly popped.

"My word!" gasped Sir Woebegone, adjusting his glasses. "Why, I do believe it's only a dummy, made of straw!"

"A dummy?" cried the King in amazement. "Do you mean to say that this is what we've been scared to death of all this time?"

"That's right!" replied Sir Archibald. "He's just a big nothin', but we let the Meanies worry and worry and worry us about him until we believed he was a real live thing!" And then he told them all that had happened on the way to the Black Rock by the sea. How the Meanies tried to stop him and how he finally found out that the dreaded Grizzlegrimm was just a dummy.

"It's most extraordinary, indeed!" sputtered Sir Woebegone. "Most extraordinary! Now if only we knew what to do about the Meanies."

"They will always be around," said Sir Archibald. "But they can't hurt you if only you do not listen to them. Just say:

> *Don't hear you.*
> *Don't see you.*
> *You're nothing to me,*
> *And how in the world*
> *Can a nothing scare me?*

Then the Meanies will fly away and that's all there is to it!"

"Splendid! Splendid!" cried Sir Woebegone, forgetting all his dignity. "I shall write it down tonight, so I won't ever forget it!"

36

Then the King arose and said, "You have done a noble deed, Sir Archibald, and we are all most grateful to you for you have freed us from fear!" And he tied a beautiful blue sash around Sir Archibald's shoulder and made him a Knight of the Order of the Great St. Bernard with crossed paws and three Golden Clusters of Elderberries! "For the bravest of the brave!" he added, and everybody stood up and shouted: "Hurrah hurrah for Sir Archibald!" It was a great day!

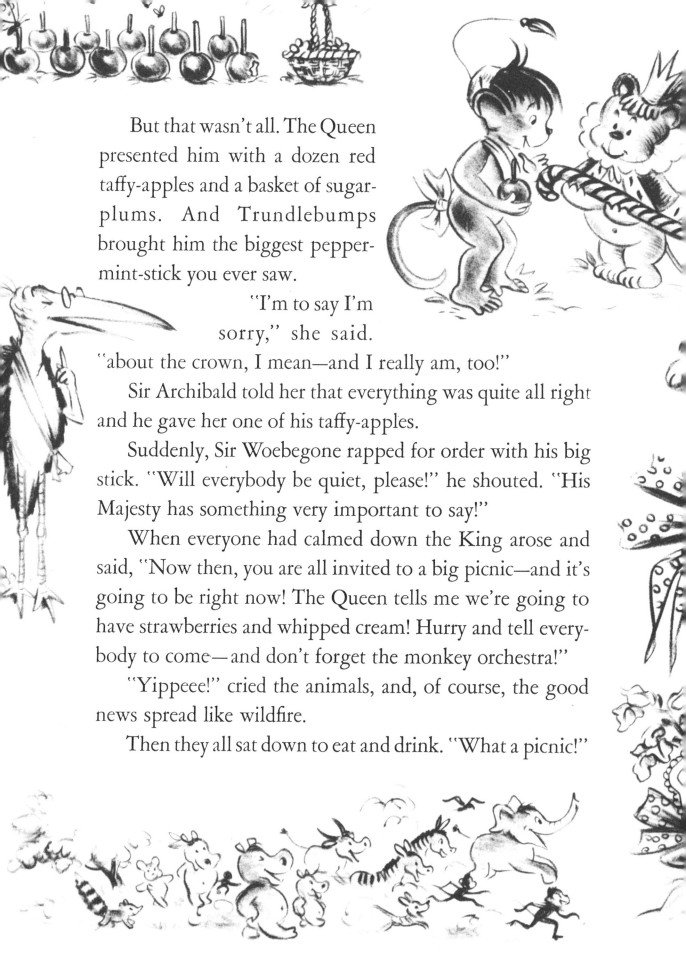

But that wasn't all. The Queen presented him with a dozen red taffy-apples and a basket of sugar-plums. And Trundlebumps brought him the biggest pepper-mint-stick you ever saw.

"I'm to say I'm sorry," she said. "about the crown, I mean—and I really am, too!"

Sir Archibald told her that everything was quite all right and he gave her one of his taffy-apples.

Suddenly, Sir Woebegone rapped for order with his big stick. "Will everybody be quiet, please!" he shouted. "His Majesty has something very important to say!"

When everyone had calmed down the King arose and said, "Now then, you are all invited to a big picnic—and it's going to be right now! The Queen tells me we're going to have strawberries and whipped cream! Hurry and tell everybody to come—and don't forget the monkey orchestra!"

"Yippeee!" cried the animals, and, of course, the good news spread like wildfire.

Then they all sat down to eat and drink. "What a picnic!"

cried Trundlebumps happily. "What food!" shouted Miss Miff. "Trouble is I never could eat very much!"

"That's too bad," replied Petunia, a hippo. "Personally I just love to stuff myself!" And turning to the Queen, she asked very politely: "Would Your Majesty mind passing the royal pickles, please?"

"It will be a pleasure!" replied the Queen. "We do want you to feel at home!" With that she poured all the pickles onto Petunia's plate.

"Thanks ever so much!" said the hippo, and she happily gulped 'em down—*plate and all*!!!

Then they all listened to the monkey orchestra, and Sir Archibald danced a most elegant polka with Floribel. When they had finished, the King and all the animals shouted:

"LONG LIVE SIR ARCHIBALD — OUR BRAVE FRIEND!" For they were all glad he had freed them from Grizzlegrimm and the Meanies!

And that is the story of
Sir Archibald and his friends.
As far as I know, they are still
peacefully living by the river
—playing together and having
a wonderful time!

STORK ISLAND

WHERE
SIR ARCHIBALD
LIVES

WHERE RED-FA
BAB

HIPPOPOTAMUSSERS

ROYAL PALACE

QUEENS GARDEN

THE RIVER

THE EERIE-WOODS

The
SCARY STUMPS →